ISBN: 979-8-218-46958-0

i

DEDICATION

Many thanks to my family and to all who've supported me
on my life's journey and tolerated my interpretation of
humor. You know who you are. And to Walt Whitman
for famously saying, "Be curious, not judgmental."

Peace

In the state of Nebraska, way out far away
past rows of tall corn stalks, beyond fields of hay,
is a small, two-room farmhouse, with an oven of stone
but no TV, no tech, no Wi-Fi or phone.

In one of those rooms
lives a girl barely ten
whose life does not stretch past
this small world she lives in.

From her mom and her dad she's
gained oodles of smarts
in subjects that span from
science to the arts.

$$X = \sqrt{(y \times y)} = ?$$

She's also learned how
to grow different crops,
and how to cook things like
bacon and tasty pork chops.

Despite all she could do –
and she did lots of things –
Amanda Sue Jones
was a sad human being.

2

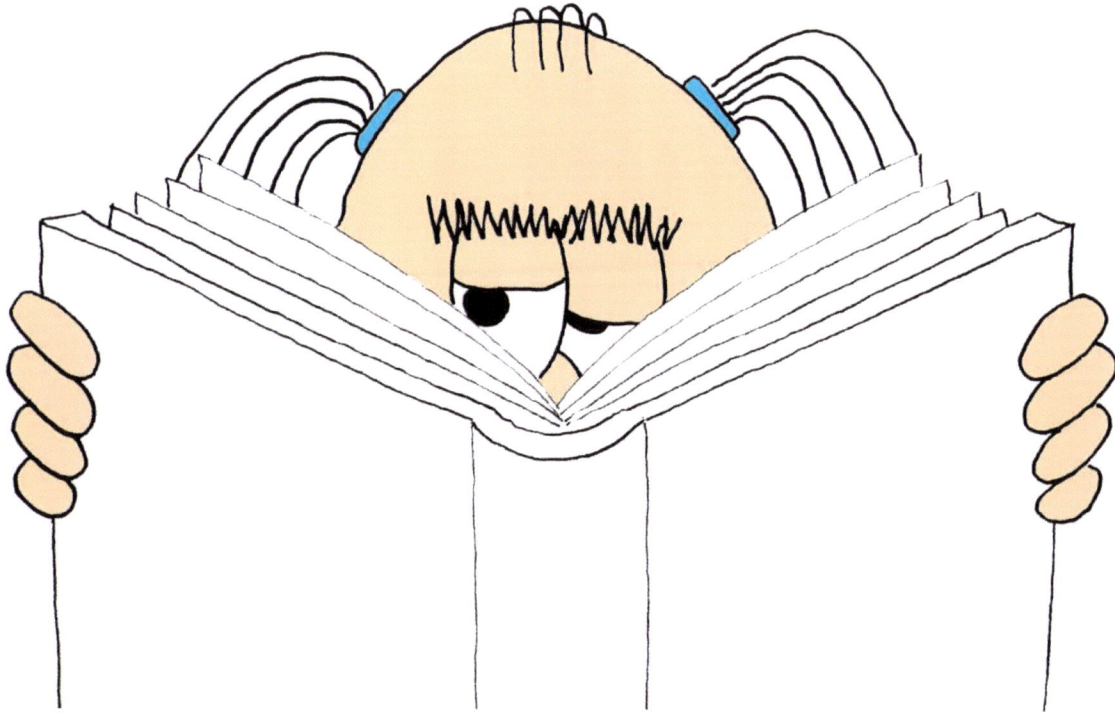

See, Amanda Sue Jones didn't much like her looks,
cuz she didn't much look like the girls in her books.

She was starting to think, though she'd much rather not,
that when it came to her beauty, she lacked it ... a lot.

Maybe her pigtails were banded too tight
or her sizeable eyebrow sometimes blocked the sunlight.

Maybe the hair in her mole grew too long
or the smell from her armpits was stinky and strong.

Maybe her teeth caused an upside-down smile
or the clothes that she wore had been years out of style.

Maybe one eyelid was a little too droopy
or the wax in her ears too incredibly goopy.

Maybe the lobes of her ears hung too low
or her nose failed to hide the mustache that would grow.

Whatever the reason, whatever the cause,
Amanda Sue Jones had a bad case of the blahs.

Her folks thought, instead, they knew what was wrong –
why their daughter was sad every day all day long.
Her appearance, they thought, wasn't what was the matter.
She was lonely and each day felt increasingly sadder.

Her mom and her dad tried
to lighten her mood.
They'd sing, they'd tell jokes,
and they made special food.

A puppet show failed, and
a magic show too.
And they once hung from
trees like two chimps at
the zoo.

Even lighthearted drawings drew nothing but sorrow.
So they'd kiss her goodnight and move on to tomorrow.

No matter the things they would say, try or do
helped Amanda Sue Jones feel less sad or less blue.

But the day finally came that would bring with it change
to Amanda Sue's world in her home on the range.

It started the same, with an orange sunrise.
But before it would end there would be a surprise.

It was just about time for the bright sun to set.
After chores and her lessons not too much was left.

That's when it happened, when Amanda Sue Jones
saw something outside that frightened her bones.
Two beady eyes that she'd not seen before
stared up and right at her through a crack in the door.

She cried out in fear, though no one could hear –
her mom and her dad were someplace not near.

But her scream did the trick,
the beady eyes fled
leaving nothing to do but to hide
under her bed.
It's there where she stayed 'til
her folks made it back.
She shared what she saw in the
back doorway crack.

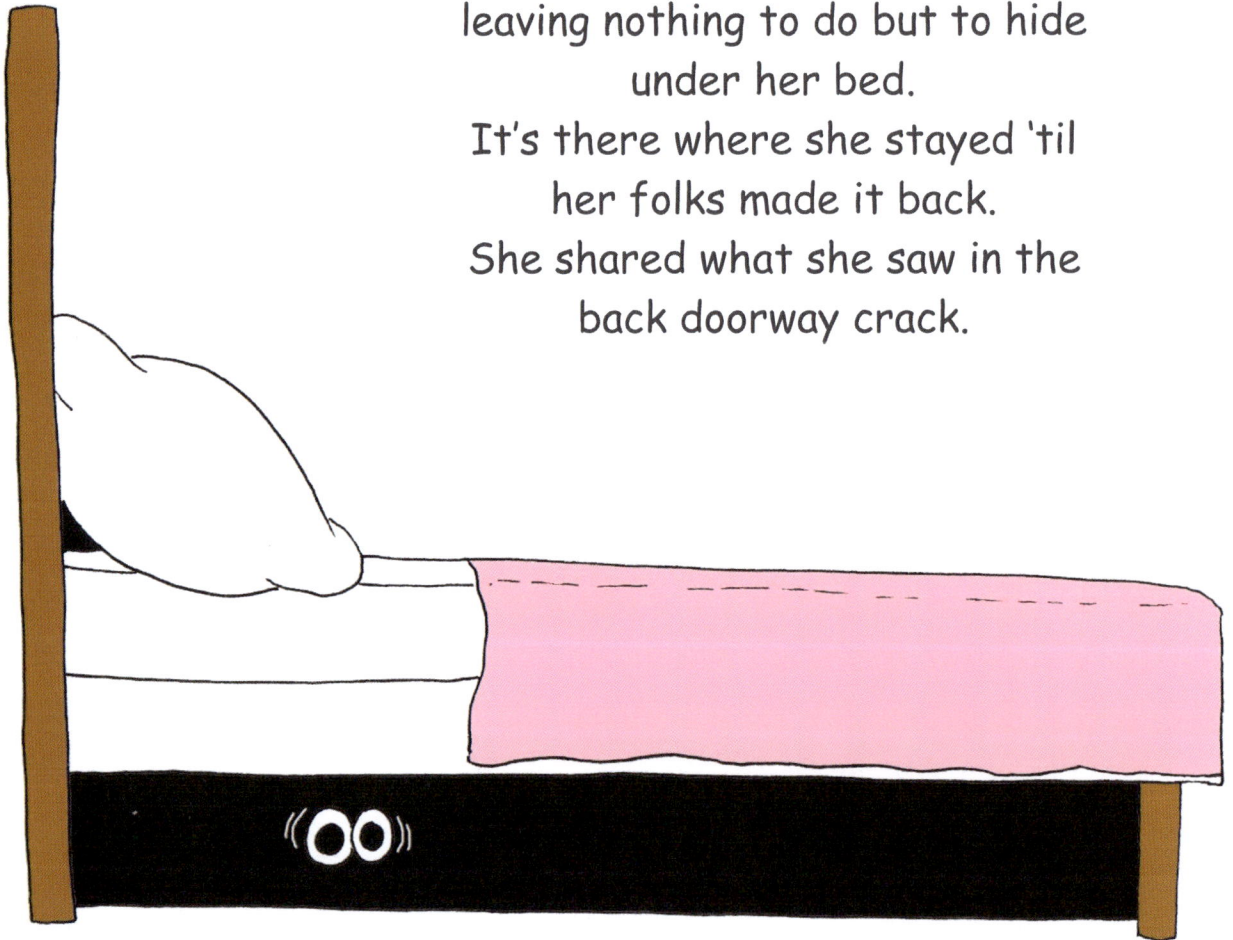

With care and with caution,
her dad opened the door
and peered into the darkness
beyond the back porch.
But all he could see was the
side of a barn
and silent dark shadows
stretching out past the farm.

A warm oatmeal cookie calmed Amanda Sue Jones.
And the three of them downed
three home-churned ice cream cones.
Then off to her bed she immediately went.
There, sleeping and dreaming were her only intent.

When morning arrived, it began a new day.
But the fright from the night had not gone far away.

In her bed, thinking thoughts of the two scary eyes,
Amanda Sue Jones feared they lurked just outside.

Not wanting to rise, but to stay safe in her bed,
she knew she'd soon have to get going instead.

For the life of a farmgirl spans past dusk to dawn,
and plenty of chores just had to get done.

So she mustered some courage,
though not very much,
and she eased out of bed 'til the
cold floor was touched.
Then she walked through the house,
which was eerily quiet,
'til she got to the backdoor where
she stood shaking beside it.
She took a deep breath and a few
deep breaths more
and reached for the knob that
would open the door.

With a turn and a push she opened it wide.
And wouldn't you know it, she was standing outside.

Her feet felt quite heavy, as if sand filled her shoes.
It took lots of effort just to get them to move.

With each step she took, fear faded away.
Her bravery grew – she could face this new day!

She went to the chickens
and fed them their feed.
Then it was off to the pigs
to attend to their needs.

She moved on to the garden and watered the plants –
taking care to not bother a hill of red ants.
The cows were next up, they got their fresh hay.
And with that she completed her chores for that day.

Heading back to the house, she held her head high –
without fear, without fret, the day had raced by.
But her mood turned quite quickly as she passed by the barn.
'Cuz a noise from within was the cause for alarm.

'Twas a growl, then a grumble then a low gurgling groan.
She thought, "What could it be," but the source was unknown.

21

Amanda Sue Jones had thoughts she should hide.
But she thought more of the barn and the noise that's inside.

She decided to see for herself what it was –
for no reason specific beyond just because.

She tried not to make any noise, none at all.
She opened a side door right beside a horse stall.

Stepping inside,
she looked all around.
Then Amanda Sue tripped
and fell hard on the ground.

The door shut behind her –
it closed on her dress.
There, sprawled like a rag doll,
our girl was a mess.

She started to cry,
just a little at first.
But soon tears filled her eyes
like a dam that had burst.

Consumed with the thought that she'd soon be attacked,
she awaited her fate lying flat on her back.

Then she heard something rustle
just beyond a hay bale.
When her head turned to see it,
all she saw was a tail.

What beast could it be at the other end of that thing?
With some courage she crawled to where it was hiding.

Peering down and behind a
hay bale she saw
a surprise – a gray cat crouched
down low on the straw.

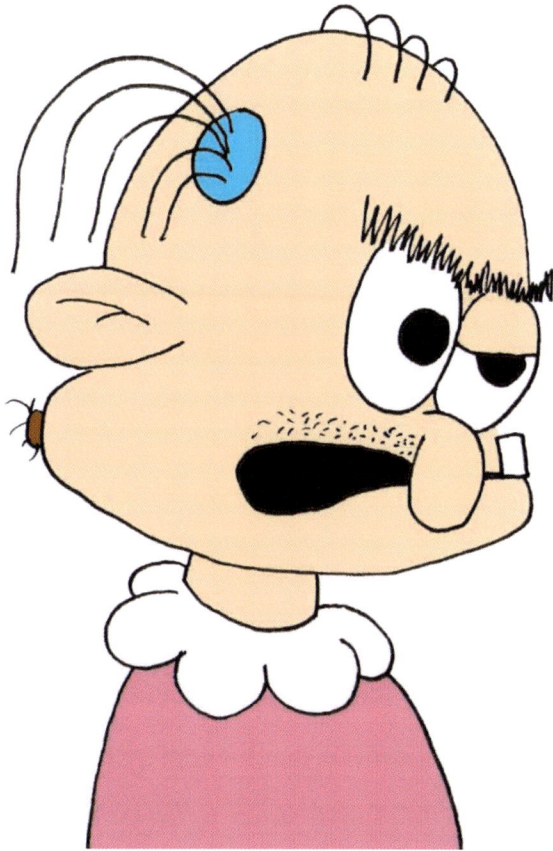

"A cat," Amanda Sue said
with surprise in her voice.
A calmness prevailed.
There was cause to rejoice.

"You're new to our farm,
I've not seen you before.
But those eyes are the
ones I saw through our
back door.

"Those eyes – they're still
frowning so meanly at me.
What could I have done?
Why are you angry?"

The cat slowly rose and backed up just a bit,
giving Amanda Sue Jones a better chance to view it.

It looked like it must be a male breed of cat.
No girl could ever look angry like that.

His fur was quite matted, his backside was clumpy.
And the hair on his head made his noggin look lumpy.

The eyes were affixed in a permanent glare
and locked on Amanda with a fierce, irate stare.

His ears sagged a bit, and one wasn't whole.
It was missing a chunk just above the ear hole.

His tail was quite crooked – it bent left and then right.
"Good golly," she thought. "This cat sure is a sight."

With two fangs sagging down from a snarling mouth,
this cat was quite angry – of that there's no doubt.

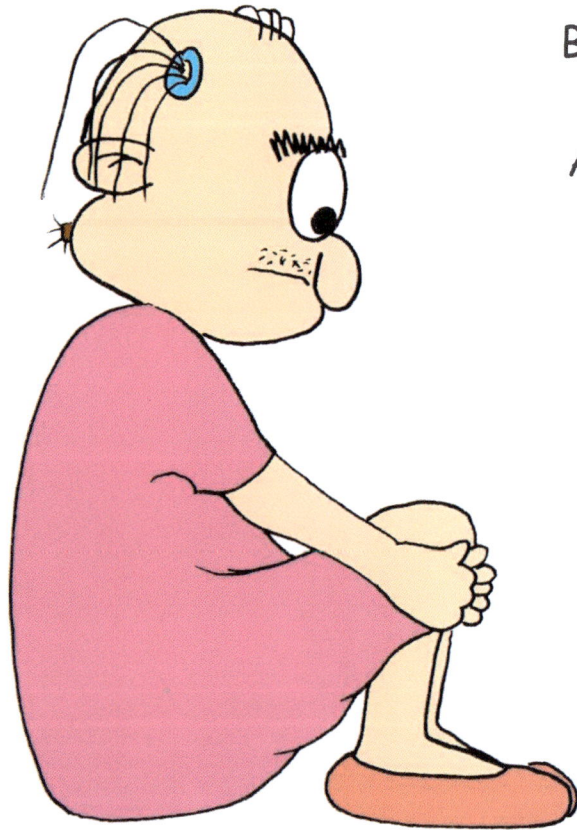

But it remained very silent,
and not once did it hiss.
An attack seemed unlikely,
she felt certain of this.

For the next hour or so the two stared at each other
'til Amanda Sue Jones heard a call from her mother.

"Supper!" was hollered, it was time to come in.
So she said her goodbyes but vowed to see him again.

She ran to the kitchen and excitedly shared
news of her great find – no detail was spared.

As Amanda Sue Jones prepared to say grace,
her mom saw the start of a smile on her face.

When supper was finished,
    leftovers were spied,
which Amanda Sue took to
    the barn just outside.

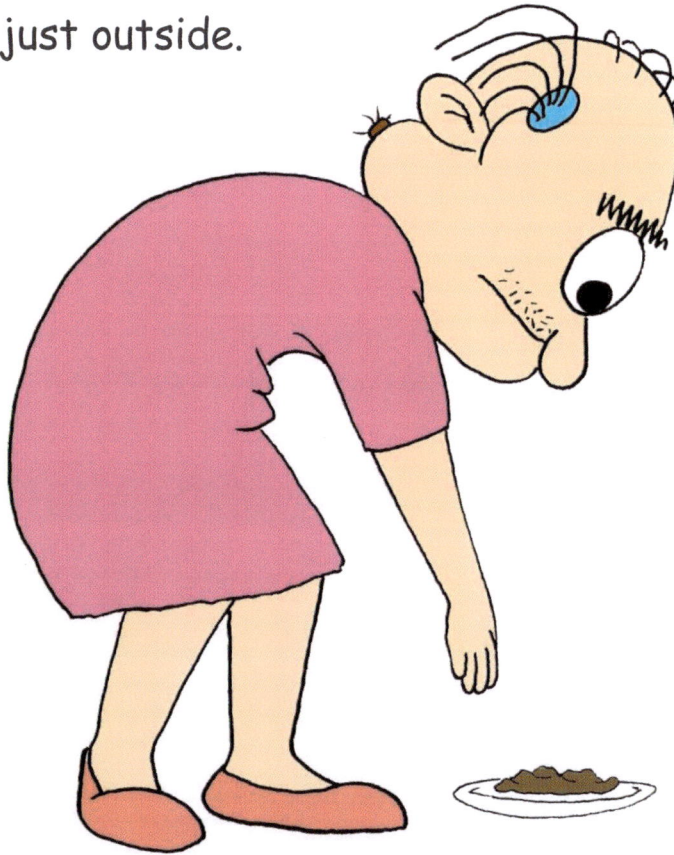

There, on a plate she placed by the side door,
she left scraps from her supper – some meatloaf and more.

Then back to the house Amanda Sue walked.
And once back inside she just wanted to talk
'bout the cat she had found just a short time ago.
Where did it come from? Does anyone know?

Then bedtime arrived
but sound sleep had to wait.
The excitement kept
Amanda Sue Jones wide awake.

When morning arrived,
there was no hesitation.
Amanda Sue Jones had
but one destination.
With the barn on her mind
and the feline inside,
she ran out to the door and
she opened it wide.

The plate she had left there with scraps from her meal
was empty, licked clean, not a crumb she could feel.

She surveyed the barn, but no cat could be found.
She looked up in the rafters, and she scoured the ground.

As Amanda Sue Jones stood there
sad and dejected
a faint sound she'd previously
heard was detected.

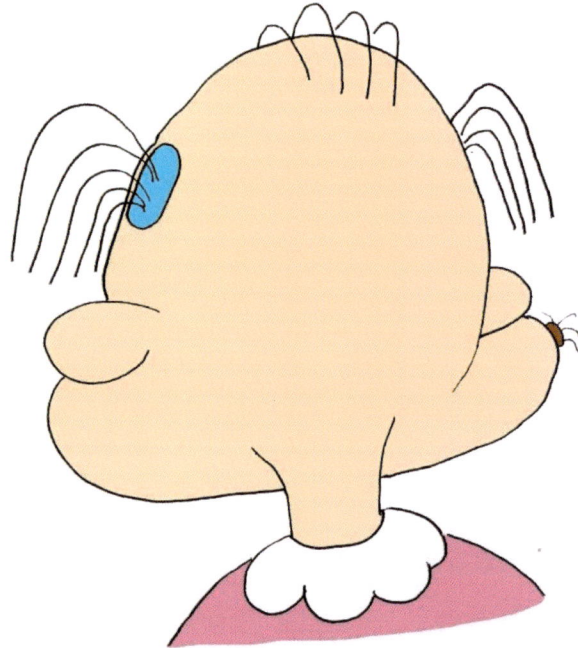

She walked a few steps and the sound grew quite loud –
like the grumbling rumbling of a thundering cloud.
A large barrel was blocking the cat's hiding place.
Behind it she saw the cat's mean, angry face.

Despite how it looked, the cat didn't act mad.
The cat looked like, perhaps, it was actually glad
at the sight of Amanda Sue Jones standing there –
standing and staring like she actually cared.

Someone caring enough to leave behind food –
who didn't just scream, who didn't act rude.

Back into the house
Amanda Sue ran
to get food for the cat,
something out of a can.

She plated some tuna and
saucered some cream
and returned to the barn
with a full head of steam.

The cat wasn't quite sure
what to make of all this.
He arched his back up
and instinctively hissed.
But his hunger was stronger
than feelings of fright,
so he eased toward the meal
and took a big bite.

Amanda Sue watched him
devour the meal,
and couldn't help thinking how
such hunger would feel.

Her parents fulfilled all her
needs, which were many.
But that cat there beside her
had no one, not any.

So right then and there Amanda Sue said,
"I'll take care of you, cat. I'll keep you well fed."

To honor her vow, she
needed permission
from her mom and her dad
to fulfill this ambition.

When she asked, they said yes
cuz they'd noticed a change –
now the mood of their daughter
didn't seem quite so strange.

So the vote was in favor of helping this cat.
A hug sealed the deal and thus ended their chat.

One thing left to do was to give her new pet
a new name, maybe something no one could forget.
She thought that the name should reflect who he was –
how he acted and looked ... from his head to his paws.

She liked the name Max,
but it wasn't enough.
It failed to reflect
his mean face and his gruff.
"I know!" she exclaimed
as his name came to her.
"'Mad Max' fits this angry,
irate ball of fur."

Not very much later
Mad Max left the barn
and moved into
Amanda Sue's house on the farm.

Weeks passed quite quickly, as did months, even years.
But change came quite slowly as Mad Max conquered his fears.

Unseen wounds from beneath the cat's fur slowly healed.
And that fur looked lots better than when he slept in a field.

A hairbrush helped also
with the tangles and knots.
Mad Max liked that too,
he liked brushing a lot.

A new diet had added a pound,
maybe two,
and transformed the cat's face
into something quite new.

Thin lips that before
left two fangs quite exposed
had filled so his mouth
was now totally closed.

Whiskers that once were quite
sparse and drooped down
now seemed so much thicker
and angled up from the ground.

Those eyes that once scared
with a mean, nasty stare
had softened and opened
with Amanda Sue's care.

And that poor mangled ear
that had been torn apart?
It healed a bit
and now looked like a heart.

If not for the tail that still
bent left and right,
one never would know this
cat once caused a fright.

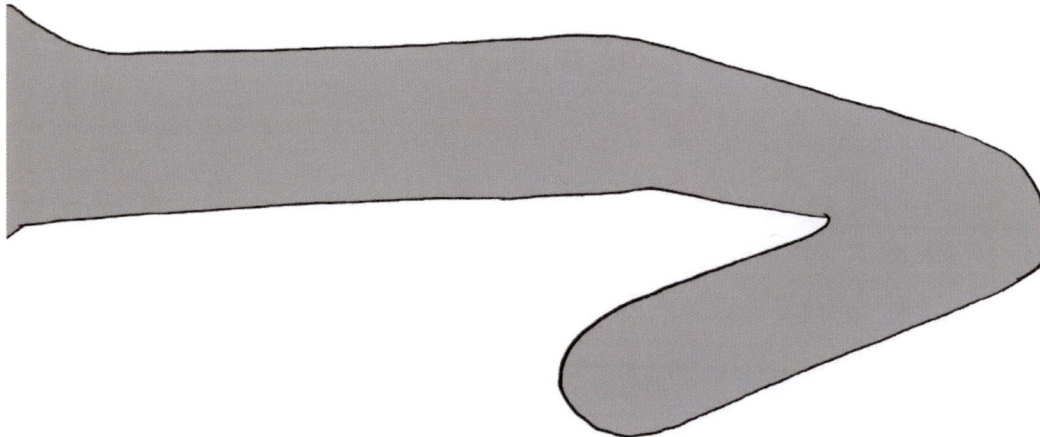

That cat no longer lived up to the name he was given.
The fear his looks caused had long been forgiven.
"Why you don't look angry or mad, not one bit.
That name I once gave you, it no longer fits."

And with that Mad Max dropped
the first part of his name.
To call this Max mad would be
more than a shame.

The years that had passed changed Amanda Sue too,
like her height – she was taller. Yes, Amanda Sue grew.

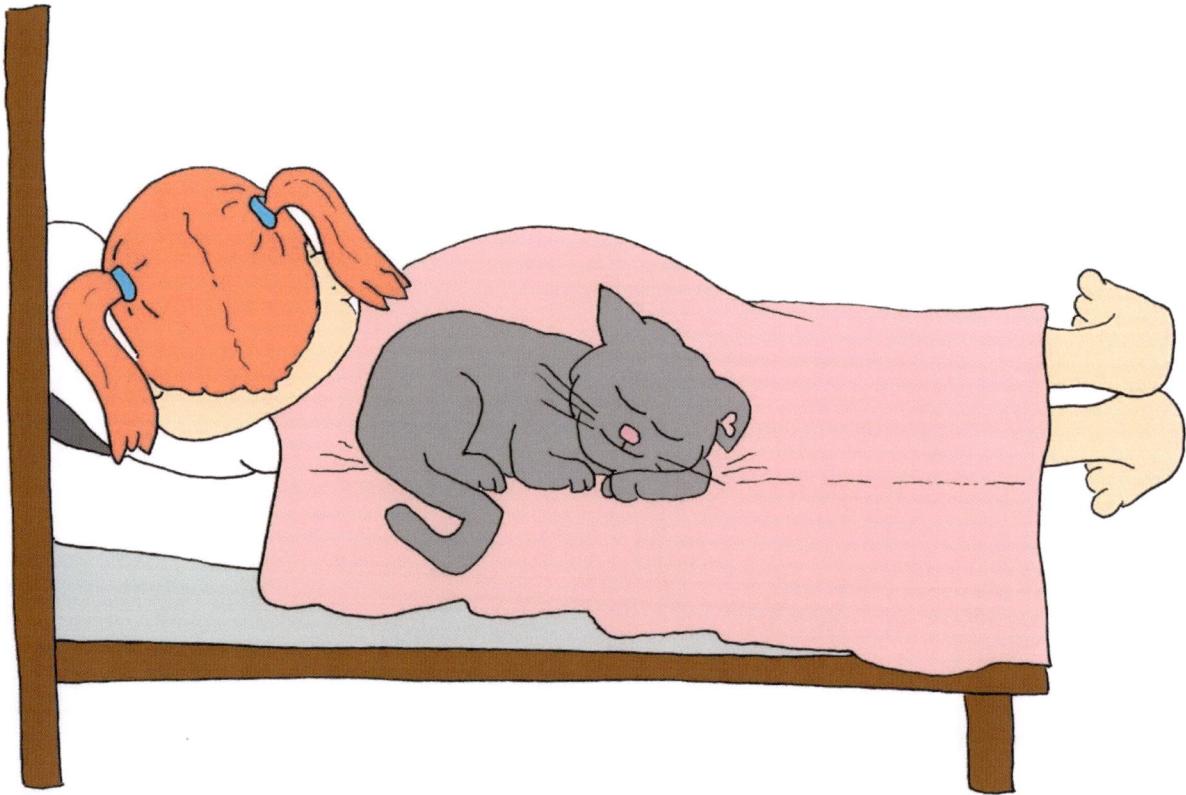

The eyebrow that once crossed both of her eyes
had parted a bit … and started to rise.

She grew lots of hairs on the top of her head,
while hairs in her 'stache and her mole were all dead.

Her lips filled out nicely and kept her teeth hid
unlike her left pupil that escaped its eyelid.

But the change that was greater than all those combined
was the grimace Amanda Sue Jones left behind.

Of course under her skin,
her eyebrows and mole,
Amanda Sue still
had a beautiful soul.
Her soul was in fact
and by far still the best,
as it was long ago when it
was put to the test.

The moral of this story is to open your heart.
And loving yourself is the best place to start.

Strangers too need more loving, not less.
No matter the number of legs they possess.

The
End

ABOUT THE AUTHOR & ILLUSTRATOR

Brian Luscomb grew up in Southern California where he honed his humor and imagination by watching 3 Stooges reruns 'til his mom sent him outside to play. He inherited his funny bone from his dad – a creative genius and talented artist who introduced Brian to the works of Charles Schulz, Chic Young and Mort Walker. (Brian discovered Gary Larson and Bill Watterson on his own.) A journalism major in college, Brian toiled in the corporate world before jumping ship to draw and write stuff that didn't need management's input or approval.

Printed in Great Britain
by Amazon